Hi, I'm
Carrie

And I'm
David

Welcome to our **Jump Up and Join In** series.

We hope you enjoy reading the books and joining in with the songs.

This book is called
Polar Bear's Big Chill.

It's lovely and it's all about enjoying the music and **relaxing**.

That's so important.
Remember to **turn the page**
when you hear th

wh-ee-ee!

Hampshire County Library
WITHDRAWN

D0543084

EGMONT

We bring stories to life

First published in Great Britain 2014
by Egmont UK Limited,
The Yellow Building, 1 Nicholas Road, London W11 4AN
www.egmont.co.uk

Text copyright © Carrie and David Grant 2014
Illustrations copyright © Ailie Busby 2014

Carrie and David Grant and Ailie Busby have asserted their moral rights.

ISBN 978 1 4052 5836 4

A CIP catalogue record for this title is available from the British Library.

All rights reserved. No part of this publication may be reproduced, stored in a retrieval system, or transmitted, in any form or by any means, electronic, mechanical, photocopying, recording or otherwise, without the prior permission of the publisher and copyright owner.

Stay safe online.
Egmont is not responsible for content hosted by third parties.

Please note:
Adult supervision is
recommended when
scissors are in use.

For all those fidgety,
beautifully different
children like ours!
– Carrie and David –

For Nick, with love.
– Ailie –

Carrie and David Grant

Polar Bear's Big Chill

Illustrations by Ailie Busby

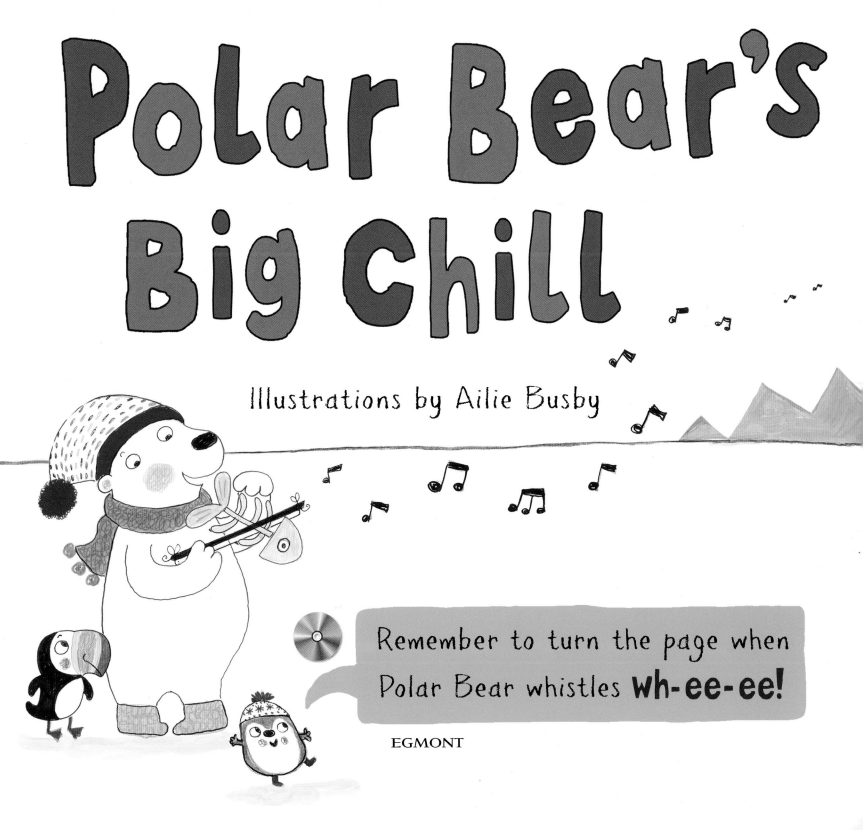

Remember to turn the page when
Polar Bear whistles **wh-ee-ee!**

EGMONT

Polar Bear wasn't very good at relaxing.

But he was very good
at fidgeting . . .

. . . and chattering

and teasing!

One day, when all his friends were having their afternoon nap, Polar Bear was feeling **fidgety** as usual.

"We're trying to relax," grumbled his friends.

So Polar Bear decided
to go hunting.

He soon came across
a fishing hole . . .

Polar Bear didn't have the patience
to fish for long but he did find
a beautiful fish bone.

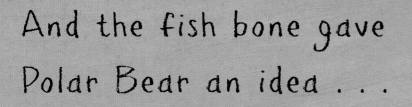
And the fish bone gave
Polar Bear an idea . . .

He tied some fishing string to each end
and made a bow out of his fishing rod.

Polar Bear put the fish-bone violin under his chin and began to play.

What a **wonderful** sound!

Soon Polar Bear's friends heard the violin's delicate music and came to see where the sound was coming from.

"Polar Bear!" they said in amazement.
"You're not fidgeting, or chattering
or teasing. You look . . . chilled!"

And Polar Bear realised that playing the violin made him feel chilled. "Let's chill out together, guys," he said happily.

And all his friends whistled soft harmonies to Polar Bear's violin playing, and the beautiful music echoed throughout the Arctic.

It was the sound of Polar Bear's Big Chill!

Oh!

I used to be a bear on the ice floe.
I moved fast but the other bears
   moved slow.
They said, "Stop!"
But I really had to go, go!
I had a dream of putting on a big show!
It wasn't that I didn't want to sit still.
It's just not the way that I wanna chill.
My beats are neat, my rhymes sublime,
And all the other polar bears
Are gonna have to keep time!

I didn't think there was a way to join in,
And then I came across some wood
   and string.
It made a sound like a heavenly choir,
And all the other bears said,
"Chilli, take it higher!"

Chorus:
Higher! (ah ha)
Higher! (come on)
Higher!
And all the other bears said, (yeah)
Takin' it higher! (ah ha)
Higher! (that's right)
Higher!

And then they said,
"Chilli, you play, we'll whistle,
    it's a new sound!"
So I played and the other bears
    came round.
It was a song that was heard through
    the land,
Chilli's violin and the Polar Bear band!

Chorus:
Takin' it higher! (ah ha)
Higher! (come on)
Higher!
And all the other bears said, (yeah)
Takin' it higher! (ah ha)
Higher! (that's right)
Higher!
Chilli's violin and the Polar Bear band!

When you play Track **7**, the karaoke track, sing along
to the whole song! Your special solo parts are in **bold**.

Lie Back and Relax!

This story was all about **relaxing**.

Music can be used for lots of things, including helping us to relax.

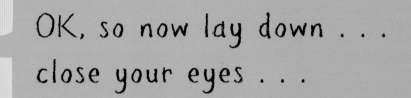

OK, so now lay down . . .
close your eyes . . .

Take some deep breaths in and out and really listen to the sound of your own breathing . . . in and out.

Peep!

It's sometimes nice to add a hum as if you were climbing stairs with the notes, going up and down.

Hummmmmm...

You can Do a Canon, Too!

So in this book we're going to move on to singing in a canon. You definitely need a partner to do this.

Let's start by singing forwards and backwards from **1** to **8** like this:

1 2 3 4 5 6 7 8

1 2 3 4 5 6 7

1 2 3

For our **Jump Up and Join In** series we really want to get children interested in music and how it works. It shouldn't be rocket science and we want to encourage you as a parent, teacher or carer to teach your children with confidence. If **you** can learn it then **you** can pass it on.

7 6 5 4 3 2 1

Now this is where it gets really clever.
The second singer should start singing from **1** when the **first** singer gets to **5**, like this:

8 7 6 5 4 3 2 1

4 5 6 7 8 7 6 5 4 3 2 1

Make your own
Chillin' Chimes!

Ask a grown-up to help you!

You'll need: Strong coathanger

Colourful ribbons   Scissors   Cord or string

Plant pots   Old keys   Corks (if you use plant pots)

Step 1 Decorate the coathanger by wrapping the colourful ribbons all round it in different patterns.

Step 2 Cut lots of different lengths of cord, as many as you have things to attach to. For these chimes you can either use plant pots from the garden or old keys – they will all work, it just depends what you have available.

Step 3 If you are using plant pots, cut a cork in half and make a hole in it. Thread the cord/string through the cork and tie a knot at the end. Thread the other end through the hole in the bottom of the pot until the pot comes to rest on the cork. Tie the other end to the coathanger.

Step 4 If you are using old keys, tie the cord/string individually on to each one at one end and tie the other end to the coathanger. The more you have the louder the noise will be! Hang your Chillin' Chimes outside and listen as the wind makes music.

About Carrie and David

Carrie and David are best known for their hugely successful CBeebies series, **Carrie and David's Popshop**. They have coached Take That, The Saturdays and the Spice Girls and have a top-selling vocal coaching book and DVD. In 2008 they were awarded a BASCA for their lifetime services to the music industry.

Parents to four children, Carrie and David are passionate about getting all children to sing and are keen to encourage adults to feel more confident in teaching their little ones music skills from an early age. The **Jump Up And Join In** series was born as a result of this passion and will help young children learn a set of basic skills and develop a real love of music. As ambassadors for **Sing Up** – a not-for-profit organisation providing the complete singing solution for schools – and judges of the young singers on BBC 1's **Comic Relief Does Glee Club**, Carrie and David believe children everywhere should be given the tools to enjoy, and to feel confident about, practising music in all its shapes and forms.

Thanks for jumping up
and joining in!
Till the next time, bye!